# Karen McCombie
# Honey and Me

With illustrations by
**Cathy Brett**

Barrington Stoke

*For Romilly (surprise!)*

First published in 2015 in Great Britain by
Barrington Stoke Ltd
18 Walker Street, Edinburgh, EH3 7LP

www.barringtonstoke.co.uk

Text © 2015 Karen McCombie
Illustrations © 2015 Cathy Brett

A CIP catalogue record for this book is available
from the British Library upon request

ISBN: 978-1-78112-475-8

Printed in China by Leo

# Contents

## Chapter 1

## I Wish

You'll think I'm mad.  But for most of this year, I've had a strange sort of wish.  I wished everything could be ... normal.

Ordinary.

Maybe even a little bit boring.

But so far, this year's been full of good luck, then bad luck.  Good times, then bad times.  In fact, any time good stuff happened, I didn't enjoy it.  Not much.  Because it meant bad stuff was lurking just around the corner.

Here's the sort of thing I mean ...

## April

❋ Mum gets a new job at the estate agents, which means lots more pay. We're rich!

❋ *The firm Dad works for goes bust and he's out of a job. We're SO not rich ...*


## May

❋ I find out that Harris Academy has a brand-new dance studio. This is the best, since I love, love, *love* dancing! It's massive with a proper wooden floor, ballet barres and mirrors everywhere.

❋ *I find out my friends Dani and Grace and everyone in my primary class got into Harris Academy – everyone except ME ...*

## June

❁ Dad's friend's cat has kittens – and Dad brings one home!

❁ *Mum goes mad at Dad cos he forgot my big brother Finn is allergic to fur ...*

## July

❁ Mum books us a last-minute surprise sunshine holiday!

❁ *But the only surprise is that it rains every day and Mum and Dad argue non-stop ...*

But maybe – fingers crossed – things are changing.

When I started at Brook City School three weeks ago, I was scared I'd be all on my own. Then I sat next to Nazreen in my tutor group, and it was as if we'd been friends for ever. (Both of us got the giggles when our teacher said his name was Mr Winterbottom. Ha!)

Then we met Scarlett at lunch. (She got the giggles when my long hair trailed in my custard. Yuck!)

And there are three other reasons that life is turning out good at my new school.

1. I like all my teachers

2. Brook City School has a great dance studio too, with huge windows that look out over the city. I can't wait to try it out ...

and

3. A cute boy called Lewis likes me, I think.

I can see Lewis now, coming out of his History class.

"Ow!" I yelp.

Nazreen has just thumped me in the ribs with her elbow. "Don't look now, Kirsten, but Lewis is staring at you!" she says.

"Yes, I know – I saw him as well," I whisper back. I can feel that my cheeks have gone pink as a prawn.

"Eek! He's walking this way!" Scarlett says.

"Pretend we're chatting," Nazreen says.

"Hey, let's chat about how much Lewis likes Kirsten!" Scarlett says.

"Shh! *Don't!*" I mutter at her.

Lewis is really close now.

"Hi!" he says. He's trying to sound all cool as he saunters past us.

"Bye!" Nazreen says.

"*Waaaaaaah-ha-ha!*" we all burst out when Lewis has gone round the corner.

We keep on laughing for ages. I hope Lewis didn't hear us – how embarrassing would *that* be?

Still, friends are more important than boys. And brand-new friends that you want to hang onto are *extra* important.

I haven't hung around with Nazreen and Scarlett for very long, but I really like them. Scarlett even looks a bit like my old friend Honey – she has the same warm smile and cute scatter of freckles across her nose.

So maybe my luck is changing. Maybe it will all be good from now on. But who am I kidding?

Good stuff is happening at school, but at home it's ALL bad news.

## Chapter 2

## Something Shocking

I keep myself pretty busy when school finishes. I've joined every after-school club there is. I tell myself it's a good way to make other friends, but there's more to it than that.

**On Monday, I do street-dance.**

**On Tuesday, it's badminton.**

Wednesday is netball.

Thursday is computer club.

And on Friday I train with the cross-country team.

Out of those five, I only really like street-dance.  So why do I do the others?  Cos I want to put off going home, that's why.

One less hour of gloom is good.

"Hi, Dad!" I call out, as I open the door on the day I saw Lewis and fell apart laughing.  I dump down my backpack of dance stuff and make my voice as cheery as I can.  I always do that, in the hope that Dad will reply in a cheery voice too.  You can't blame me for trying.

"Have you seen your brother?" Dad bellows.

Uh-oh.

Sometimes Dad is gloomy because he still hasn't found a new job.

Sometimes Dad is gloomy because he and Mum have had a big row.

Sometimes Dad is gloomy because Finn has got in trouble at his 6th-form college.

"I haven't seen him," I say, and I go into the living room. "What's wrong?"

Dad is hunched over the computer. The phone is clutched tight in his hand.

"I've just had *another* call from his form tutor," Dad says. "That's three calls in three weeks!"

He rubs his eyes and looks totally fed up. The last two calls were to say Finn had been missing classes at his 6th-form college. They said he wasn't doing his work and he was mucking around and being cheeky to teachers. I suppose this call is the same.

So Dad is stressed and Finn is in big trouble. But I can't think of anything to say to make things better, so I go and give Dad a hug.

"What's going on with your brother, Kirsten?" Dad sighs. "He was always such a good boy ..."

"Mmm," I mumble in reply.

'Finn isn't the only who's changed,' I think to myself. Dad didn't used to be this miserable all the time.

"Hi!" Finn yells, as he comes in and slams the front door shut.

OK, it's time for me to hide out in my room. I love my brother and I love my dad, but they don't like each other very much at the moment. It's no fun to hear them tear shreds off each other.

Anyway, I just saw something shocking on the computer screen.

Mum and Dad haven't been getting along for months.  But is Dad ... is Dad planning to move *out*?

I could see from the screen that he had been looking at a flat for rent in Willow Road! Willow Road is on the other side of the park, near where Honey lives.

I haven't seen Honey in *such* a long time.  I wish I could be in the park with her now, sitting on the swings and chatting like we used to.

That's what we'd do when life was simple and sweet for Honey and me.

## Chapter 3

## Keep Calm

"Got time to come back to mine?" Scarlett asks the next day.

We've just got out of school. For some reason, the teachers were feeling kind today and they didn't give us any homework. Tuesday badminton got cancelled because the P.E. teacher is off sick. I haven't been to Scarlett's house, or Nazreen's yet, so yes, it's really nice to be invited back to her place. Sounds like fun.

"I'd love to," I tell Scarlett.

There's something else I'd like to tell Scarlett, and Nazreen too. We've had lots of laughs together so far, but best friends are there to share your problems with, aren't they?

And I so need to talk to someone about how horrible things are at home.

"Hey, check this out," Nazreen says. She's been staring at the screen of her mobile. She flips it around and shows us an image on Instagram. It's one of those "Keep Calm" things.

"Keep Calm and Wish Your Troubles Away," Scarlett reads aloud.

"It's from my old friend Jade," Nazreen says. She rolls her eyes. "Jade loves posting stuff like this. She was always moaning about her life. I'm kind of glad she went to a different secondary school!"

I nearly trip over my own feet when Nazreen says that.

Now I don't feel like I can off-load my problems after all. I'd better keep calm ... and keep quiet. From what Nazreen's just said, if I grumble about Mum and Dad and Finn then maybe I'll scare off my new friends.

"Hey, I just remembered," I say to Scarlett. "I'm so sorry, but I have to get home. I can't come to yours today. Another time, yeah?"

"Aw," Scarlett says, and she pulls a sad face.

I wave to her and Nazreen and run off. I run and run, in the hope I can leave the lonely feeling behind – but I can't. I run and run till I find myself at the park. My heart is beating fast from the burst of exercise – and from lying to my new friends.

But then, with the green of the grass and trees all around, I start to relax. Kids are skipping and playing and goofing around, which makes me smile. I loved this place when I was little like them.

I see that the swings are empty, and so I plonk myself on one, and I think of Honey.

We used to come here all the time after nursery. Mum sat and read or chatted to the other parents, and Honey and me would scramble onto the swings. We'd giggle like crazy, and kick our legs high in the air.

We were almost like twins back then, never apart. Honey would always be by my side at story time, or hold my hand when we went out into the nursery garden to play.

Then we stopped being so much like twins ... and it got harder to see each other cos Honey didn't go to my primary school.

And when I made friends with Dani and Grace, I only saw Honey every now and then. I'd still meet up with her sometimes at the park. We'd sit and sway on the swings together, catching up and swapping stories. But that hasn't happened for, well, *years* now.

'How is she?' I wonder. Will she still look the same? Her skin was the colour of honey and her tight, curly hair was too. She'd smile so much that her freckly nose would crinkle.

Then I remember something.

The tree in the corner of the playground – it has a hidey-hole in the trunk near the bottom. Honey and me, we used to pretend that fairies lived inside.

On days I didn't see Honey, I'd leave notes in there for her. When I was small, they were just funny little doodles. As I got bigger, I'd try to write a proper note. Stuff like – "*Can yo met me at 4, Hunny?*"

A girl and her mum over by the pond look at me and smile, and I realise I just laughed out loud.

Then I have an idea ... I pull my school journal out of my bag and tear a page out. I

use my best purple pen to scribble something
and run over to the tree.

There's the hidey-hole, same as ever. And here I am, tucking my note to Honey inside.

Honey won't find it, I know, but it gives me a warm fuzzy feeling just to do this, as if she's almost here with me now.

And hey, if she *does* find it?

Won't she be pleased that now I'm 12, *at last* I can spell her name right!

## Chapter 4

## In a Spin

It's Wednesday, and I've missed netball club to come to the park. (No loss – I don't exactly love it.)

I feel silly as I sit here on the swing in my blazer and tie, waiting for a girl who won't show up.

It's been so long that I can't be sure Honey lives around here any more. Even if she does, why would she look in the hidey-hole in the tree? Maybe I should just go home and –

"Boo!" says someone I can't see.

Two cool hands come from behind and cover my eyes. For a second I'm scared – till I hear

a giggle I know so well, even if it's been years since I last heard it.

"Honey?" I say. I can't believe my luck. "Is it really you?" I'm so shocked that my voice comes out like a tiny mouse squeak.

Honey lets go and comes around the front of the swing. She's tall now, but apart from that she looks exactly the same. She's even wearing a short dungaree dress that's like a cute, more grown-up version of the little kid outfit she always used to wear.

"Course it's me, you numpty!" she says. "Thanks for your note, Kirsten. It was a nice surprise."

Honey flops onto the empty swing beside me and her curls bounce around her face in that old super-cute way.

It's *so* lovely to see her.

"I didn't know if you'd look in the hidey-hole," I say. "I just kept my fingers crossed and hoped you would!"

"I check it once in a while. Just in case," Honey says with a smile and a shrug. "So how are you? How's Dani and Grace?"

"Oh, I don't see them any more," I tell her.

"Is that OK?" Honey asks, and she starts to spin around on her swing.

"It's OK," I reply, and I begin to spin around too.

Dani and Grace are nice, but we weren't friends so much, even before they went to Harris Academy and I went to Brook. They were both in the swimming squad and they spent every spare minute training. When I did get to see them, they'd have damp hair and goggle marks round their eyes and nothing to talk about but speed drills.

"I'm glad to hear that," Honey says, then she lifts her feet and spins fast in the other direction. "Whee!"

I giggle and do the same. We're all grown-up now, but spinning like this makes it feel like it was yesterday that the two of us used to goof around on the swings together. But then – as we come to a stop – I do something silly.

I start to cry.

"Hey, Kirsten!" Honey says, and she reaches out her hand to me. I take it.

We gently sway together. She says nothing and waits for me to talk first.

"Sorry," I say with a sniffle. "Things are a bit difficult at home."

"Why?" Honey asks. "What's been going on, Kirsten?"

At first, the words I want to say stick in my throat, but then I blurt them out.

"I think my parents are going to split up," I tell her.

It feels so horrible to say it out loud – perhaps that's why I've never done it before.

I expect to feel bad ... but I don't.  Not really.  Isn't that funny?

Now that I've got the words out there it feels all right.  It's like when you're stressed about a test, or a visit to the dentist, and then it isn't so bad when it actually happens.

"That's so sad," Honey says.  "Do your mum and dad know how upset you are?"

"No," I say, and I shake my head.  "I don't want to make things worse."

"You silly sausage!" Honey says with a giggle.  "If you keep worries secret it makes things worse, Kirsten.  If you talk about them it makes things better."

Her giggles float like bubbles all around me. Just being with Honey makes me feel brighter, lighter.

And I just remembered – when I was small I told Mum that Honey was as lovely as a glass of lemonade. It made Mum laugh ... but that really is what Honey is like. Sweet and bubbly, an instant hit of happiness.

Then I think of how life is now, with Dad all flat and gloomy and Mum always busy and cross.

"It's too hard," I tell her. "I don't think I can find the right words to say. And I'd get too upset saying them. I just feel stuck."

Honey looks at me with her kind eyes and giggles again.

"Kirsten, you don't have to speak out loud, do you?" she says and then she holds something up. It's the note that I wrote her.

That's it!

*That's* what I need to do.  Write down my feelings in a letter.  Two letters in fact – one each for Mum and Dad.

"Got some paper?" Honey asks.  "Get on with it then!"

I grab my homework journal out of my bag and smile.  When I was scared and shy at nursery, Honey came along and made everything better.

Is she going to do the same for me now?

I think perhaps she is.

# Chapter 5

# From Bad to Better

I had a good day today. Here's why ...

❋ On the way to school this morning I bumped into Dad's friend Glen, and he showed me pictures on his phone of the kitten we couldn't keep cos of Finn's allergy. She looks like a proper little scamp and so happy in her new home.

❋ There was a notice up in the dance studio to say that our street-dance team is taking part in a big competition soon, which is pretty exciting. New moves, new costumes and maybe even a prize. I can't wait!

❀ Nazreen and Scarlett made a plan for us all to go and see a movie this Saturday afternoon. (Great – I thought they might not ask me after I bottled out of going to Scarlett's on Monday.)

❀ Even computer club was fun – and Lewis joined! We didn't speak (not properly, not yet), but he said my app design looked cool when he passed by my screen.

And now here I am outside the front door of our house, biting at my lip.

Yesterday, Honey made me think that writing down my feelings was the best thing to do. Now I'm not so sure, and I have this sense of dread pressing in my chest. Mum and Dad should have found their letters by now. Before I left for school this morning, I tucked Dad's under the keyboard, so he'd spot it when he switched the computer on. Then I popped

Mum's in her handbag while she was off in a flap looking for her keys.

Dad's letter is in a blue envelope, Mum's is in a yellow one, and both are covered in kisses. Both letters say the same thing.

**You two seem very angry with each other all the time, and I feel very muddled and upset. I go to bed worrying and wake up worrying. Please can you tell me what's happening? I would rather you told me than feel like I do now.**

**Love you lots and lots, Kirsten x**

How will my parents respond? I'll find out what Dad thinks first. But Mum won't be home from work till after six.

I take a deep breath and walk in.

"Dad?" I call out in a shaky voice.

"In here, Kirsten."

Oh, he must be in the kitchen. That makes a change. Dad's usually on the computer in the living room, looking for jobs – and flats.

I walk into the kitchen and am surprised to see that Dad's not alone.

"Hello, darling!" Mum says, looking up from the table.

Finn is sitting next to her and he's frowning.

"OK," my brother says to Mum and Dad. "Now Kirsten is here, can you get on with this 'family meeting', or whatever you want to call it?"

"What's going on?" I ask.

"Here, Kirsten," Mum says with a smile, and she pats the chair next to her. "That was a

brave thing you did. Dad and I got your letters, and you're right. We need to talk. We all need to talk."

Yes, Mum is smiling, but her eyes look sad. She and Dad are about to tell us bad news, I'm sure, but I don't mind. That horrible sense of dread has gone and I'm oddly happy.

Like Honey said, secrets only make things worse.

And if Mum, Dad, me and Finn can all talk, maybe things will start to get better.

# Chapter 6

# The Best Thing

When I get to the park, Honey is swinging back and forth, and it looks like she's singing to herself. She hasn't seen me yet and I'm glad. I have a gift for her and I don't want her to spot it.

"Ta-nah!" I say as I run towards her across the springy surface of the playground, with my schoolbag thudding against my hip.

I take the bunch of sunflowers from behind my back and hand them to Honey.

"Wow!" she gasps. "No one has ever bought me flowers before."

"Well, I went into the supermarket for a bottle of water after school and I saw these on special offer. I *had* to buy them for you – as a thank you."

"So, the letters did the trick?" she asks. She looks pleased for me.

"Yes. Mum and Dad talked to us yesterday," I tell her as I sit down on the next swing. "We had a family meeting and it was really hard, but they told me and Finn everything. They said how difficult this year has been and how they haven't been getting on, but they're sorry – they didn't realise how bad it's been for us."

"So do you think things will get better?" Honey says.

"Mum and Dad promised to talk about their problems together, instead of shouting at each other," I tell her. "And they promised to think of my feelings, and Finn's too."

"That's really good, Kirsten," Honey says. "Was Finn OK about it?"

Ah ... Finn.

Mum, Dad and me all said that we felt tons better after our chat, but my brother just got mad.

"Finn stormed off," I tell her. "He ran out of the house and slammed the door and didn't come back till late. I tried to speak to him this morning, but he told me to leave him alone – only he wasn't as polite as that!"

I look over at the sandpit where me and my brother used to play together. My favourite ever photo of us was taken there – I was four and Finn was nine. He'd made me the best sandcastle ever and then I went and kicked it over, like little kids do. Finn didn't get cross – he burst out laughing! In the photo, he has this huge, wide smile and I'm grinning too, happy that whatever I did pleased him so much.

I wish we could laugh together now.  I
wish I could talk to him properly, and find out
what he's thinking.  But it's like he's on some
different path and has left me way behind.

"Text him," Honey says, as if she can read
my mind.  "Ask him to meet you here."

"What?" I say.  "No way will Finn want to
hang out at the swings with me."

"Rubbish," Honey says, and she makes her
voice all strict.  "I bet he'll come.  You just need
to meet outside of the house, away from your
parents."

She's right.  It's a fab idea.  But that's Honey
for you – she always knew the best thing to
do.  When we were little she'd see when I was
worried, and nudge me to go tell the nursery
staff.  When I felt lonely, she'd lead me to
other kids and we'd join in their games.  When
I needed a wee, she'd take me to the loo, so I
didn't have an accident.

"I'll do it!" I say, and I tap out a text on my phone.

*Ping* – it's sent.

"Finn is only angry cos he's upset," Honey says. "He just needs more time to get his head around it and –"

Honey doesn't get a chance to finish – a text has pinged back from Finn. It says –

**OK. Near park now. See you in 5?**

"Told you!" Honey says with a grin. "I'll leave you to it."

"I'll write you a note and tell you how it went," I say as she waves and walks away.

"Sure – stick it in the tree," she calls back. "Good luck!"

When she's gone, I look over at the swing she was sitting on and see she's left her sunflowers there.

## Chapter 7

## Wrong or Right

"Kirsten!" Nazreen says. She looks really pleased to see me.

She and Scarlett are sitting at a table in the new ice-cream café across from the park gates. They'd asked me to come with them, but I told them I had plans to meet an old friend after school today.

"Didn't your friend Honey turn up?" Scarlett asks. She moves along the bench so there's room for me to sit beside her.

I nearly tell them what happened.

That I went to meet Honey, but *she* left and my brother came to meet me instead.

45

That I tried to talk to Finn about Mum and Dad and what was going on, and he got mad AGAIN, and stormed off AGAIN.

This time, Honey got it *wrong*.

"She had to go," I tell them instead. It's easier to say that than tell the truth.

"Never mind," Nazreen says. "Here – see what you fancy!" And she passes me the menu. It has lots of ice-cream flavours on it, but I'm too upset to choose anything.

"Ooh, those are pretty, Kirsten," says Scarlett. She's noticed the sunflowers I'd put down on the table beside me. "Who are they for?"

"For my mum and dad," I say from behind the menu.

That's true, at least. If my parents are trying to make things nicer at home, then I will too.  Since Honey doesn't need her sunflowers, I decided they'd look lovely on the kitchen table. Like a blast of happiness and sunshine.  And we'll need that, if my brother is being a black cloud.

"So which one are you going for?" Nazreen asks.  "The Toffee Crunch is *so* good.  Try mine!"

I look up and see Nazreen holding out a spoon.  I lean over to taste her ice cream – and spot someone peering in the café window.

It's Finn!

He's spotted me, and he rushes inside.

"Hey, Kirsten," he says, and he pushes his dark hair away from his face.  "I'm so sorry I ran out on you just now."

"Don't worry," I tell him.  "Are you OK?"

Finn's face is flushed, and he's all restless, shuffling his feet.

"Look ... I've hated this year, Kirsten," he blurts out. "I've messed stuff up at school. And at home. I've just been so angry."

Out of the corner of my eye, I see Nazreen and Scarlett staring. They're wondering who this 6th-form boy is and what he's on about. But I'm not going to interrupt Finn now, not when he's talking about how he feels at last.

"I mean, all these months I was sure things were terrible between Mum and Dad – but I wanted to be wrong," he carries on. "I wanted them to be OK. And now they've told us they *are* having a hard time ... I'm just sad. And a bit scared, to be honest."

I realise that he's still standing up, so I budge along and make space for him, and Finn flops down beside me.

"It'll be OK in the end," I tell him. "One way or another."

"Yeah," he says. "I guess. I just need time to get my head around it."

It's what I told him in the park, before he stormed off. And it's what Honey said to me first, of course. Hey, maybe she got it right, after all?

"Sorry!" Finn says. He's only just spotted that I'm with friends. "Didn't mean to barge in on you guys!"

I need to introduce everyone, don't I?

"This is my brother Finn," I begin. "And Finn, these are my friends Nazreen and Scarlett."

Finn grins and nods a hello, and Nazreen and Scarlett blush a bit and smile shy smiles back.

Finn turns on the charm. "Good to meet you," he says. "*You* look normal – and smell normal too!"

Nazreen and Scarlett frown at each other and giggle.

"What do you mean?" Nazreen asks.

I want to know too. What's my brother on about?

"Kirsten's last friends were like fish," Finn says. "They were always swimming. They carted wet costumes and towels around with them everywhere they went. Our house stank of chlorine every time they visited!"

Nazreen and Scarlett giggle some more, and I join in. Finn has always been funny. Even teachers used to love him. Till this year, when 'funny' turned into 'cheeky and difficult'. But I suppose that was just cos he was so unhappy.

Maybe now he's talked to me – and Mum and Dad – he'll change back to funny Finn. I hope so.

"And her other friend, the one Kirsten had back in nursery school … well, *Honey* was pretty special, wasn't she, Kirsten?" Finn grins at me.

I freeze, colder now than the melting ice cream in front of Nazreen and Scarlett.

"Don't, please," I whisper to Finn. But my voice is so low he doesn't hear.

"What was her full name again, Kirsten?" Finn asks. He scratches his head as he thinks. "Oh, I remember," he says. "It was Princess Honeyblossom Cupcake!"

"What?" Nazreen says. She frowns at Finn, then at me.

"What kind of name is *that*?" Scarlett asks.

"Well." Finn laughs. "Don't you think Princess Honeyblossom Cupcake is a great name for a –"

I can't stay. I HAVE to get out of here, *now*. I know what Finn is going to say next, and I can't stand it.

He'll say that Princess Honeyblossom Cupcake is a great name for an imaginary friend ... and Nazreen and Scarlett will think I'm totally mad and never want to hang out with me ever again.

"Kirsten? Kirsten! Come back!" I hear Finn yell as the café door bangs shut behind me.

But I'm not going back. I am fuming. How dare he do that to me in front of my friends and ruin everything? Now it's *my* turn to be cross and upset and storm off.

## Chapter 8

## One Last Thing

The two chains above me are twirled together tight. I look up at them and get snowflakes in my eyes.

"One, two, three, *WHEEE!*" I say, and I lift my feet off the ground. I giggle as I spin around fast, then wobble to a stop.

A little girl in a padded yellow coat and fluffy mittens stops and stares at me. I'm a crazy big girl sitting on a swing on my own, laughing to myself.

But I don't care. I grin back at her and wave.

I was on the way from Dad's new flat to meet my friends at the cinema, and I realised I could take a shortcut across the park. So here I am, taking a few minutes to think about stuff.

It's nearly the Christmas holidays, and so much has happened since the day I ran out of the ice-cream café.

For a start, Mum and Dad split up at last ... but they did it with no shouting, and they're trying to be friends, for my sake and Finn's. For everyone's sake, in fact – the shouting was making us *all* feel rubbish. The day Dad moved out we all cried and hugged, but it's been good since then. Mum's always busy dashing to and from work, but home feels much more calm and peaceful now. Dad got that flat in Willow Road and it's really cool. He's back to his happy self – a lot less stressed out and chuffed cos he started a new job last month.

The street-dance team trained like crazy for weeks and, in the contest yesterday, we came 2nd out of 15 teams.  It was such hard work, but I loved every minute of it and we all got to show off the cup we won at Assembly this morning.

The friends I'm going to meet … well, that's Nazreen and Scarlett, of course, and Lewis too. Me and Lewis started to walk home together after computer club and we've become good mates.

And Finn?  He's back to being funny Finn, and there have been no more phone calls from his 6th-form college.  Best of all, me and my big brother get along brilliantly again.  We chat when we go to and from Dad's place.  We talk about all sorts of stuff, all the time.

How strange is that?  Not so long ago, I kept dark, uncomfortable secrets cos I had no one to tell them to.  And now I have Finn and Mum and Dad, as well as Nazreen, Scarlett and Lewis.

There's no Honey to talk to, of course. There never has been, not really. I made her up when I was little and sad, and I made her up again a few months ago when I was bigger and sad.

At least Finn didn't tell Nazreen and Scarlett what kind of friend Honey was in the end. The day I panicked and ran from the café, I didn't hear how he finished his sentence. I was worried that what he was going to say was – "Don't you think Princess Honeyblossom Cupcake is a great name for an invisible friend?"

But *in fact* what he said was – "Don't you think Princess Honeyblossom Cupcake is a great name for a little kid to make up?"

So Nazreen and Scarlett thought it was just a cute pet name I made up for my best buddy at nursery. Like it's cute that little kids believe in the Tooth Fairy, or think unicorns might be real.

My sweet and special secret is safe. And it really is one that I'll keep to myself!

But there's one last thing I need to do now. I jump off the swing and walk over to the tree with the hidey-hole. I fold the note, give it a kiss and stick it in there.

Honey – thank you for everything.

Your forever friend,
Kirsten x

Yes, she might not be real, but she was there – sort of – when I needed her.

I'll always think of us, Honey and me, swaying, chatting, laughing on the swings together.

Forever friends.

# Also by *Karen McCombie* ...

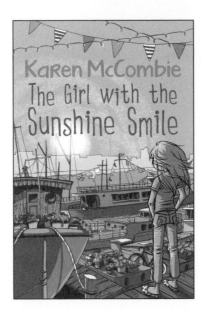

Meg is the girl with the sunshine smile ...

That's what they call her at the wedding fairs where she models her mum's dresses. But then Mum meets Danny.

Danny, with the grotty houseboat, four sons, and a three-legged cat. All of a sudden, Meg's life clouds over.

Will Meg ever find her sunshine smile again?

www.barringtonstoke.co.uk